THE DEVI~~L~~ ~~S~~ ~~SEED~~

A DETECTIVE INSPECTOR TAYLOR SHORT STORY

PHILLIP JORDAN

FIVE FOUR PUBLISHING

Get Exclusive Material

GET EXCLUSIVE NEWS AND UPDATES FROM THE AUTHOR

Thank-you for choosing to read this book.

Sign-up for more details about my life growing up on the same streets that Detective Inspector Taylor treads and get an exclusive e-book containing an in-depth interview and a selection of True Crime stories about the flawed but fabulous city that inspired me to write, *all for free.*

Details can be found at the end of **THE DEVIL'S ELBOW.**

Chapter 1

"GIVE IT ANOTHER minute will you, woman?"

Detective Sergeant Doc Macpherson gave an imploring look before tugging his jacket sleeve down to rub a porthole in the steamed-up driver's side window of the old Volvo.

"Are you frightened the ghouls are going to get you?"

Macpherson snorted in reply.

A westerly wind was driving the rain down the street in sheets but it was doing little to deter a coven of tiny witches going door to door in the annual search for coin and confectionery.

"It's not Halloween until the weekend for God's sake," he added with another grunt of derision and a shake of his head.

Macpherson reached forward and tweaked the control of the Volvo's heater in an attempt to clear the windows. It responded with the gasping gurgle of an asthmatic on eighty a day.

"Ack, come on, will you?" He thumped a palm on the dash, his huge paw at odds with the rest of his stature which had earned him the moniker of one of Snow White's famous

4

friends.

"It's easing off. Let's get this over with and I'll shout you a Maharaja on the way back," said Detective Inspector Veronica 'Ronnie' Taylor, wielding the knowledge that naan bread and lamb biryani were more effective than carrot and stick in motivating the man who, since the death of her father, was much more to her than subordinate and colleague.

Before he could answer, the boom of impact caused them to jump in their seats, the heavy metallic thuds striking from the rear quarter panel to the driver's door sending their hearts into throats.

"Trick or treat!"

Macpherson heaved his door open.

"Get away home, you wee bastards!"

The scurry of feet and a riot of laughter drifted in the wake of the disguised youths as they sprinted away, black capes and devil horns disappearing into the gaping black mouth of the entry that ran behind the row of old Victorian terraces and down to the footpath cutting along the edge of the Stranmillis Embankment.

"You alright?" said Taylor, stepping out into the mizzle to join her sergeant.

"Near gave me a bloody heart attack."

He wasn't wrong. It wasn't too long ago two police officers, in this part of town, would have been a target for the local gunmen.

Taylor closed the Volvo's door and turned towards number seventy-four. Inside the bay window was framed with ominous black drapes and the soft scarlet glow of candlelight.

"Trick or treat," said Macpherson with a tut, following his inspector across the road and up the broken tile path.

Taylor reached out and thumped a brass goat's head against scratched paintwork.

Trick or treat, she thought, eyes coming to rest on the children doing their rounds. Their sing-song requests ringing out as each door opened to spill light onto doorsteps and eager outstretched hands.

The simple tradition and rhyme brought darker thoughts to the forefront of her mind. Memories of her father out on the beat and the worry of her mother. The echoes of television bulletins and the scent of newsprint. The shadow of Northern Ireland's troubled history was never far away, and with only a few days to go until the anniversary of the Greysteel massacre, those three simple words conjured up images of carnage and cruelty.

Her mind was still preoccupied as the door to number seventy-four Brunswick Street creaked open.

Inside the house, the heat was stifling.

Three gas bars grinned from the grate and there were enough church candles burning in close proximity to voile and velvet that even the usually composed Taylor felt the creep of anxiety.

Macpherson was sweating bullets. He dabbed his brow with the cuff of his jacket, trying and failing not to look aghast at the menagerie of mismatched furniture, Celtic idolatry, crystals, and the wall-mounted lamb's skull.

Their host it seemed was oblivious to his shock.

"Please. Sit yourselves down, can I get you tea? Are you not soaked."

"We're grand, Mrs Meehan," said Taylor.

"You can call me Luna," she said, waving away Taylor's formality and ushering the two police officers towards a sofa covered in gaudy throws and a coating of pet hair.

Taylor eased onto the edge while Macpherson resisted, his eyes scanning the room for the beast responsible.

"You've a cat?" he said.

"I've a few." Luna nodded, her eyes wrinkling ahead of a sage nod. "I can sense you're not a cat person."

Macpherson sat hesitantly beside his inspector, drawing up his cuff to show a ragged scar.

"I'm not a fan of anything that sinks its teeth in for no good reason. Give me a goldfish any day of the week."

The householder gave another bob of the head. "There's always a reason," she said cryptically.

Luna Meehan was probably pushing sixty but looked younger. She had clear skin and her straw-coloured hair was tied back from a pale narrow face. In contrast, she wore dark eyeliner and lipstick which gave her a slight air of theatricality when combined with the purple taffeta skirt and a long frock coat. As she moved nearer the hearth Taylor noted she was barefoot. At first glance and with the addition of a pointy hat, the woman wouldn't have been too far out of place going door to door with the kids outside.

"You reported some suspicious activity by the river?"

prompted Taylor.

"I did. I did." Luna held up a palm and then retreated out of the room into what Taylor presumed to be the scullery.

"Ack, she's a spacer," mumbled Macpherson.

"Shhhh." Taylor nudged him with her elbow.

"Have you seen thon?" He stabbed out a finger to make his point.

"Yes." Taylor had seen the sideboard with its collection of crystal balls, bones and Ouija board.

"And she's a soup merchant."

A bottle of gin was tucked discreetly beside the room's only armchair. Empty glass by its side.

"Here we are." Luna breezed back into the room and presented a small wooden trinket box inlaid with Mother of Pearl.

Taylor's brow furrowed in confusion.

"I got it at the charity shop," Luna gestured vaguely out the bay window. "Across the bridge, beside the surgery."

Taylor nodded, aware of the row of shops but unable to recall exactly which one Luna referred to. Luna thumbed a switch, illuminating the room's big light to better appraise the piece.

"Were you on your way back when you saw something?" said Macpherson.

"Oh no." The woman gave an emphatic shake of her head.

"No?" Taylor gripped her knees so as not to run an impatient hand through her hair.

"Not in that way." The woman caressed the box solemnly.

"Mrs… Luna," Taylor smiled. "What exactly do you need us to look into?"

"A death, inspector. An untimely death."

"I'm sorry, I—" Taylor began, eyebrows rising at the sudden revelation.

"I've seen her every night since I brought this home."

"You've seen a ghost?" breathed Macpherson, unable to keep the scepticism from his tone.

Luna gave a patient nod.

"It's easy to mock what we don't understand," she said, offering the box to Taylor.

It was in good repair, the hinges glistening as though they had been recently oiled.

"Her name is Julie, or Jenny," said Luna. "Or Judy?"

"Jesus, at least you've narrowed it down to an initial…" Macpherson's words were barely audible under his breath.

"How do you know that?" said Taylor, ignoring him and looking up.

Luna shrugged.

"I see her in the water, by a bend in the river near a bridge. She's calling out her name."

"Luna, I appreciate you might think that you've—"

"I know what I see, inspector. My abilities and the prejudices of those who can't comprehend them are not new to me." She knelt and placed her hand on Taylor's. Her touch was warm and oddly comforting. "I'm not asking you to understand, inspector. I'm asking you to open your mind because somewhere out there a mother is wondering what became of her daughter."

Taylor looked again at the box but there were no distinguishing marks. She clicked open the lid.

And the lights went out.

Chapter 2

"IT SMELLS LIKE the devil's armpit," said Detective Constable Chris Walker, trying and failing to mask the stench with the crook of his elbow.

"It can't be that bad." DC Erin Reilly shooed her partner away from the trash heap.

"Have you been into the gents the morning after Doc's been for an all-you-can-eat?" Walker took a step back, taking a deep cleansing breath. "I have and I'll tell you what, this comes in a close second."

Reilly swatted away a squadron of bluebottles. It stank right enough.

"I'd have thought the constabulary had more pressing matters to attend to. Do you want me to dig you out a couple of shovels and you can lend a hand?"

Reilly rose from her haunches and nodded a greeting to the council worker plodding through the fly-tipped pile of split bin bags, rotten garbage, household junk and general wanton waste.

"A criminal offence is a criminal offence," said Reilly as he stopped a few paces short and nudged a pile of broken bathroom tiles away from the kerb with his boot.

Morning traffic rushed past, buffeting them in the slipstream. There was little of interest to the commuters, the waist-high mound not gratuitous enough to warrant the slow creep of rubberneckers.

"Ever since the depot started limiting what goes to landfill this carry-on has been on the increase. Norman Murphy." Murphy gave a polite nod of introduction to both officers, leaning on his shovel and surveying the mess.

"Did you report it?"

Murphy bobbed his head. He was a small man, five foot five and slight in stature, his head bullet shaped with a covering of steel grey fuzz.

"To the office, like. I didn't phone nine, nine, nine."

Reilly brushed off her hands and sighed. There wasn't much more for them to see, and there was no more they could do other than log the location details and keep an eye out for any witness reports that came in. The council would inform them if anything incriminating was found in the contents.

"Not as bad as last time," said Murphy. Reilly raised a questioning eyebrow.

"Waste fuel and oil drums."

"Where was that?" said Walker, taking a quick step into the detritus to avoid the wing mirror of an onrushing bus. The council worker gestured over his shoulder.

"Up near Drumkeen Forest. We had the environment agency and fisheries involved too. They thought it might

12

have contaminated the water." He thudded his shovel into the pile. "My boss is spitting nails over the head of this."

"Yours and ours both," said Reilly.

Illegal dumping was on the rise and it was impacting the crime statistics for the quarter which in turn meant the chief super was on the warpath over the league tables, and like the garbage spilling across the embankment, his anger also rolled downhill.

"Are you taking it back to the depot?" she said.

Murphy gave a grunt.

"Eventually. We'll have to wait on a supervisor before we sift through it and see if we can identify where it might have come from but there's that many cowboys it could end up being from all over the city, further maybe."

"Someone got it lifted," said Walker. "Probably paid for it too. "

"Aye, and if there's anything to identify them, and they point the finger, then it'll be over to you to track down the culprits." Murphy smiled but without confidence anyone would be caught. His expression changed.

"Davy, be careful. There could be syringes or anything in there. What are you doing?"

Ten feet away his younger colleague who had been carefully circumnavigating the heap had bent from the waist to dig his hand through a pile of what looked like old clothes, sweat-stained pillows and crumpled bedsheets. Davy was tall, rangy and pale as a corpse. He couldn't have been more than late teens, very early twenties.

"I just thought..."

Murphy excused himself and tramped over, face reddening.

"Get out of it. Leave looking for anything until George gets —"

Reilly and Walker had followed and now watched as Murphy knelt and plunged a gloved hand into the waste at the boy's feet.

"Not quite a diamond in the rough, but..." He offered his open hand to Reilly.

"Distinctive," she said.

In his rough gloved palm, the council worker held a pendant on a snapped chain. The decorative charm was silver and fashioned to resemble an ornate mirror with a black cat perched on the lip.

"Not the sort of thing you'd turf out." Walker peered over Reilly's shoulder, then to the boy. "Good spot."

Davy blew his jet-black fringe from his eyes and shuffled, staring at the ground towards the spot from where his treasure had been seized.

"Flip it over?" said Reilly, not really sure what she hoped to see. Murphy nudged the piece over. The back was smooth with a hallmark stamp below which was an engraving.

Just the two letters, J.W.

Chapter 3

THE CID SUITE at Musgrave Central took up a section of the building's eastern facade, the blast-proof windows overlooking Ann Street and across to the Queen Elizabeth Bridge, the Lagan Weir and beyond that the dome of the Odyssey Complex and the famous Belfast shipyard, birthplace of the Titanic and home to its twin cranes, Samson and Goliath.

The area was divided up like any modern office space with blue fabric acoustic screens marking out workspaces, rest areas and meeting zones, each territory distinct and yet, as Taylor walked towards the area which housed her small team she noted someone had been busy adding a touch of spooky adornments to all.

Decapitated pumpkin heads lined the sills and artificial cobwebs clung to the corners of windows. Among the cubicles, cardboard skeletons rattled their chains and at least half a dozen rubber bats dangled from the suspended ceiling tiles.

Cutting across the central aisle she caught sight of

Macpherson outside the rest area of section two.

"Here she is. Doc's telling us all about your encounter with the 'Witch of Brunswick'." Detective Inspector Phillip MacDonald dropped a set of bunny ears around the description, his expression creased in amusement.

"And you weren't to know Sergeant Harris would have us out chasing ghosts, I suppose?" said Taylor, swinging her bag from one shoulder to the other.

MacDonald laughed again and swept his chair around to face the other man in the room. Tall, tanned and immaculately groomed, Detective Constable Samuel 'Slick' Simpson offered her an embarrassed shrug.

"You're not the first if it's any consolation," he said.

Taylor waved the apology away. In the past, she had dismissed the DC for his egregious oiliness and his enthusiasm to impress superiors and those of the opposite sex. The frost had thawed though when they worked a domestic violence case together.

"What's her story?" said Taylor. MacDonald slid his chair up to his desk and leaned on his elbows.

"Fruit cake. Every major enquiry she's on the phone wanting to lend her 'services'." He dropped the bunny ears for a second time.

"She's a medium," said Simpson.

"You should be in tailoring with an eye like that, Slick," said Macpherson.

Simpson smiled. "A psychic."

"What was it this time?" asked MacDonald.

"Spirit of a dead girl needing justice," said Taylor, ushering Macpherson towards their own desks.

MacDonald waggled his fingers and gave a wavering woo, his laughter following them as they left.

"It's not like you to turn your face up at buns?"

Detective Constable Carrie Cook pulled back a Tupperware box of iced cupcakes topped with ghosts, pointed hats and pumpkins.

Macpherson raised a steadying hand. "Hang on now, not so fast there, DC Cook." He beckoned the box back and Cook relented. "I'm still feeling a bit ropey from last night's kebab but one of these should sort me out." He didn't look certain and Cook shook her head as half the cupcake disappeared in one bite.

"Guv?" she said, offering the box.

The DC had initially been seconded to the team during the investigation to a domestic slavery ring but with a workhorse ability to get the job done and an inherent aptitude for investigation Taylor had managed to keep her on board, much to Macpherson's delight due to her endless supply of home-baked cakes and savouries. Cook was a feeder.

"Thanks." Taylor plucked one out and placed it on her desk. DCs Reilly and Walker approached bearing tea and coffee.

"Thanks," Taylor echoed accepting her coffee from Reilly. Walker deposited his drinks to Cook and Macpherson, taking his own from Reilly. He lowered his nose to his shoulder and sniffed.

"Run out of Right Guard or something?" said Macpherson, washing the second and final bite of cupcake down with his tea.

"I can still smell that crap from this morning." Walker gave a shudder, then self-consciously reached up to brush his hair forward as all eyes looked at him.

"More fly-tipping?"

"Along the embankment near the Lockview and the forest park."

"Shitting in the same place twice. That's not too far from the fuel spill," said Macpherson.

He nodded up at the map of the city and surrounds pinned on their display board. Twenty coloured pins had been jabbed through the printout into the cork marking different sites.

A red pin skewered a section of the River Lagan near the Belfast Boat Club and the fringes of the Lagan Meadows nature reserve and Drumkeen Forest Park. It marked a lethal section of fast-flowing water known locally as The Devil's Elbow, a spot which had claimed multiple lives from thrill-seeking canoeists to those foolish enough to think it could be forded on foot.

"They're getting bolder," observed Cook.

"CCTV in the area?" asked Taylor.

"Down. There was a power cut last night," said Reilly

Macpherson spluttered a mouthful of tea. "Don't talk," he said mopping a splash from the desk with his cuff.

"What happened, did you get lost on the way to the bathroom?" said Walker with a grin. Macpherson pulled a face.

"The power went off in the middle of an interview, and then I had to drive around for half an hour to find a kebab shop still open. The Maharaja had to close early," Macpherson's head wobbled in irritation as he thought back to missing out on a visit to his favourite takeaway restaurant.

"You could do with skipping the odd midnight snack, sarge." Reilly lunged forward and prodded him in the midriff.

"You can't fatten a thoroughbred, Erin," he scolded, batting her hand aside.

"I'm surprised you were still hungry after your scare," said Taylor, easing back into her seat and peeling the cupcake case off.

"What scare?" The three DCs said in unison.

"Ack, don't you be encouraging them, Ronnie."

"Is this about the wicked witch of the west?" said a voice.

All heads turned to face the newcomer rounding the cubicles. Constable Leigh-Anne Arnold gave a cheery smile. The TETRA radio attached to the lapel of her hi-vis jacket warbled and she turned it down.

"Brunswick is more south than west, Leigh-Anne. If you'd stayed in school you would know that," grumbled Macpherson. Arnold's blue eyes twinkled in her baby face.

"We were responding to a call about suspicious activity; let's say the lady had a flair for the dramatic and the power cut added to the theatre of the evening," explained Taylor. Arnold chuckled accepting a cupcake from Cook.

"She sees dead people," said Arnold.

"Piss off," said Walker, eyes widening.

"I'm just telling you what they say."

"The only spirits she sees are supermarket own brands," said Macpherson, crooking a finger at the box of buns.

"Guv?"

Taylor gave a Walker a dismissive wave. "I think the spirit of the season is getting to everyone," she said. "What can we do for you, Leigh-Anne?"

Arnold balanced her cupcake over the case, nibbling icing off the top.

"Sergeant Harris says the council have turned up some stuff might be of interest on the fly-tips."

"Okay, thanks. Erin, can you and Chris see if it's a viable lead so we can report some progress to the chief super?"

Reilly nodded and gave a thumbs up.

"There's something else too, guv. I'm just back from a call-out reporting a historic domestic incident."

Taylor nodded and dug out her notebook.

"The reporting party is Helen Broadbank. Her friend hasn't shown up to their last two arranged meetings and she thinks she may be a victim of coercive control."

"So it's out of character?"

Arnold nodded then gave a little wince. "They are part of a paranormal society."

"You must be joking me," said Macpherson, letting his forehead slump to the desktop.

"Have we a name for the friend?" said Taylor.

Arnold was skimming through her notes.

"I have it here somewhere…" she said, mumbling as she chewed the last of her bun. "Josie, Jamie, Jacqui…"

Chapter 4

"HUBBLE, BUBBLE, TOIL and trouble, huh?" said Macpherson, clipping in his seatbelt.

Taylor pulled the Volvo's door closed and waved out of the window at the three chalk-white faces staring from the doorway of the student accommodation that doubled as home to Pentangle Paranormal.

"They seemed sweet enough."

"They want to tell their faces will. Between the make-up and the metal, they'll scare the bloody ghosts away, and your woman in the middle? Did she have fangs?"

Taylor chuckled.

"Takes all sorts, Doc."

"There's something in the bloody water this week," he huffed, nudging the Volvo into traffic.

The girls had been welcoming although certainly, they were unique in their physical appearance and hospitality.

All were dressed resplendently in blacks and deep purples, Marie did indeed have fangs, and Helen Broadbank had enough piercings in her ears and face to sink the Titanic, but to Macpherson, the cranberry tea served in skull-design mugs on a coffin-shaped coffee table had definitely upped the ante from odd to borderline cuckoo.

Broadbank had explained to the two detectives that not all of her 'sisters' could attend but that the three of them; herself, Marie Faux and Caroline Duggan could vouch that Jane Morrow who was a founding member of their group had disappeared and cut off contact just after their last "summoning", the evening culminating in an altercation between the girls and Jane's boyfriend, Maxwell Parker.

"They probably wanted to use him as a human sacrifice," said Macpherson, swinging the Volvo across traffic and onto Ormeau Embankment.

The road was hemmed in on one side by skeletal branches overhanging the wrought iron railings of Ormeau Park, the oldest municipal park in the city and former home of the second Marquis of Donegall until mounting debt saw the land sold off to the Belfast Corporation.

On the other side, the grey-green waters of the Lagan silently continued their journey from the slopes of Slieve Croob out to Belfast Lough.

"It'll do no harm hearing his side," said Taylor as Macpherson turned right across the Ormeau Bridge and then left into an avenue of three-storey red-brick terraces.

"Aye, I just hope as he doesn't open the door dressed as bloody Dracula."

"I've give him a shout. He'll be down in a minute. Just grab a…"

The young man who'd identified himself as David Black and had granted them access to eighty-eight Cairo Street paused and had the courtesy to blush as he gestured towards a rickety sofa and two beanbags.

"Was anybody killed in the explosion?" said Macpherson, surveying the damage.

"Sorry, got a bit carried away last night." He shrugged. "Just sit wherever you can find a spot," he said, pulling on a dark parka jacket with a fur-lined hood. "I'm running a bit late for work here." He gave an apologetic smile and picked up an armful of the dozen or so empty pizza boxes, and moved to crack open the blinds and the window.

"I'll let a bit of air in," he said by way of apology for the fug of body odour and the less than wholesome fragrance of the morning after the night before.

"No problem," said Taylor moving to wait in the middle of the small lounge for Parker to make an appearance.

"Students," said Macpherson doing a three-sixty as the letterbox rattled declaring David's departure. "Might as well be Dracula we're visiting. The wee shits sleep all day and wreck all night."

Tobacco and the scent of Class Bs clung to the fabric in the room. So did the smell of stale lager and fried onions and the decor did little to deter the stereotype of student lads more keen on excess than education. A pyramid of beer cans was stacked on the hearth, the grate itself packed to the gills with discarded fag packets, sweet wrappers and junk mail. Separating the lounge from the kitchenette, a glass-topped table was topped with mug ring marks and an overloaded ashtray, alongside a pack of playing cards and scattered copper coins.

The kitchenette wasn't in a much better state. The sink overflowed with crockery and cutlery, while sat on the worktop was the obligatory stolen traffic cone and a mug tree festooned with mismatched underwear.

Macpherson huffed out a breath and prodded one of the beanbags with his toe.

Taylor watched Parker's housemate dump the boxes into a wheelie bin and then cross the street, glancing back as he walked away.

Cairo Street, like its neighbours, Damascus, Jerusalem and Palestine made up a section of the lower Ormeau known as The Holy Lands. Built by the Victorian developer and former Lord Mayor of Belfast, Sir Robert McConnell, the names had been inspired by his travels to the Middle East.

The rows of red-brick terraces once housing working-class families had now largely been snapped up by property speculators, sub-divided, and then given over to student accommodation. The result during term time was a wild riot of endless parties and anti-social behaviour.

The thump of a baby elephant hammering down the stairs drew her attention away from the window. The young man who entered was wiping sleep from his eyes with one hand and wrestling his hair into shape with the other.

"Hi," he slurred, fighting the effects of a rude awakening from a hops and barley induced slumber.

"Maxwell Parker?" said Taylor.

"Max," he nodded at Macpherson who stood at parade ground ease with a stern expression. "Dave said you're the police. Is this about the party?"

Parker negotiated the room's mess to search the kitchen countertop and then a cupboard for a clean glass. Not finding any he rescued one from the muddy waters of the sink.

"It's about Jane Morrow."

"Oh."

"Do you want to sit?"

"I'm alright here," he said testily, setting down the glass and folding his arms.

"Is Jane here?" said Taylor.

"Pfft, what would she be doing here?"

"You're her boyfriend aren't you?"

Parker shook his head. "Not anymore."

"Not after you hit her a slap in front of her mates, eh, son?" said Macpherson.

"I didn't hit her—"

"Three eyewitnesses say different."

Parker pointed a finger, his voice rising.

"If anyone was in the wrong it was those crazy bitches, she —"

"Easy, Mister Parker, that's quite a temper you've got there," said Taylor.

Parker dropped the finger and eased into a non-threatening stance. Two seconds later he was barricaded behind folded arms.

"Do you not care about what her mates were up to? You should be looking into that?" he said.

"We are interested in Jane's whereabouts as there has been a concern raised regarding her safety," said Taylor. She remained in the centre of the lounge, tempering her annoyance at Parker's belligerence with the knowledge he was dying with a hangover.

"If you think it's just charms and chants for the craic, I'm telling you different, that Helen one is twisted."

"Just focus, sunshine," pressed Macpherson "What about Miss Morrow? Do you know where she is?"

"When I went round, the crazy bitch was boiling mice! Boiling them alive and making Jane join in for Christ's sake!" Parker had become agitated and pushed off the counter, pacing the kitchenette in obvious distress at the memory.

"You don't look like the stereotypical animal rights activist," said Macpherson. He raised a hand up in a measure of Parker. The young man was pushing six feet, probably close to fifteen stone and was built like the wall. The Ulster rugby shirt he wore strained at the biceps and shoulders and there was no doubt that he was well accustomed to a T-bone steak.

"It's just wrong. She's sick," he mumbled.

"Max," said Taylor. "Rather than lash out at Jane's friends can you just tell us if you know where she is or the last time you saw her?"

Parker rubbed his face. There was a creak in the hall that was impossible to miss.

"Sorry." David Black walked sheepishly into the lounge, crossing to the sofa and shoving his hand down the side of the seat. "Van keys, I didn't mean to interrupt."

Taylor gave a small shake of her head to say he hadn't and then Black retreated, the slam of the letterbox once again declaring his departure.

She watched him walk away. This time he didn't look back.

"I don't know where she is, honestly," said Parker.

"And the last time you saw her?"

"Look, after… after what happened, she stayed away for the night. The next morning she came back to gather up what stuff she had here and left. She didn't even speak to me. She just left."

"You didn't try to get in touch?"

"Not right away, I thought she was with…" He stopped, face reddening and unable to speak the name of the Pentangle Paranormal Society.

"But you tried later?"

"Yes, to apologise, but she must have blocked my number."

"Did you try other friends, her parents?"

"No, she didn't have many mates before those girls got their claws into her and she told me she didn't really get on with her folks, Bible bashers according to her. Tried to keep her wrapped in cotton wool. We weren't together long enough for me to ever meet them."

"How long?"

"A couple of months."

Taylor took a breath and cast an eye around. Observing

him in his home environment, she thought she had the measure of him. Big guy, sporty, popular with the lads and the lasses alike. The house was obviously party central and was unquestionably a male-dominated lair. Booze, booty, and the PlayStation all confirming her initial feelings that university for Parker was more social than scholarly.

A few months wasn't long enough to count as a serious relationship but had he been drowning a broken heart or had he sailed on with a clear conscience.

"What are you studying?" she said, turning her attention back to Parker.

"Structural engineering with architecture."

"Was Jane at uni?"

"Biological sciences," said Parker nodding.

"Okay, Max." Taylor nodded, indicating that the questioning was over for the moment. "We'll be back in touch. You're not planning on going anywhere are you?"

Parker shook his head and she placed a business card on the marked surface of the table.

"If you have any sudden recollections or insights as to where Jane might have gone, give me a call."

Chapter 5

APPROACHING THE CID suite, Taylor and Macpherson found that the entrance was now guarded by four foot long, skull-faced grim reapers suspended one on each side of the door.

The puppets' red eyes were illuminated and their haunting moans and the rattle of chains followed as they pushed through the doors. Macpherson paused to plunge a hand into a disembodied plastic pumpkin head to retrieve a fistful of roasted monkey nuts.

"Best thing about bloody Halloween," he said with a grin, offering one to Taylor.

Cook and Reilly were sat at their desks, each busy at their respective keyboards, and Walker was pulling printouts from the copier.

Macpherson wrinkled his nose as he sat down.

"What's that smell?" he said through a mouthful of nuts, dumping the shells on the desk.

Walker's eyebrows rose and he gave his arm a long sniff.

"What's it smell like?" he asked tentatively.

"That smell is hard graft, sarge," said Reilly, rising to her feet and pulling a face.

"Come off it, Tinkerbell, you two wouldn't know hard graft if it hit you up the hole."

Reilly flicked a broken shell across the table, hitting Macpherson on the chin.

"On the contrary," she said. "We might have our first firm lead on the fly-tippers."

Walker presented the contents of the copier with a flourish.

"Two hours of my life I'm never getting back spent poking through a council tip comparing piles of garbage." He shuddered. "To think some people choose that as a job!"

"You're a copper, Chris. Dealing with other people's crap is your job." Macpherson spun a couple of nuts across the table at his two juniors. Walker considered his words as he cracked open the shell.

"What do you have?" said Taylor, accepting the offered printout.

"The council stored the last three dumps and the effects from The Devil's Elbow fuel spill at their Blackstaff compound. In summary, they identified comparable material from each dump site, mostly commercial but also some domestic."

Taylor looked at the snap-shots of garbage piles and then individual items and finally several rows of documents that had been carefully laid out on a workbench.

"We canvassed the people at those addresses and each confirmed they had paid for waste removal. Two are from the south side of the city and a third was out near Newtownabbey and the dates match the tipping to within twenty-four hours," said Reilly.

"None of them admit to knowing it would be fly-tipped but all of them used the same contractor, Junk It. They found him on Facebook."

"Happy days, well done." Taylor gave a nod of gratitude for the effort and then Reilly grasped the nettle of bad news.

"Unfortunately the Facebook page no longer exists and the phone number associated is dead. We do however have a partial plate for a white van with a distinguishing mark on the rear driver's panel."

"Okay, I take it you're running the partial for a match."

Walker nodded. "We've put in the request and it's running now."

"Okay, good. What about the mark?"

"Ghosting," said Reilly, widening her eyes and waving her fingers at Macpherson.

"I'll ghost you in a minute," he grunted mid chew, one cheek puffed out like a squirrel with toothache. Reilly snatched another nut from his pile.

"The previous decals have been removed and the paint underneath the vinyl stands out against the remaining sun damage," said Walker. "We don't know what it says but the fact each of the people we spoke to mentioned it, narrows down our suspect vehicle."

"And with more than sixty per cent of used vans being white, you may get that crackpot medium back on the phone for a bit of help," said Macpherson.

Walker looked a little deflated after the appraisal.

"It's a start," said Taylor. "More than we had this morning. Good work."

Macpherson harrumphed at the approval and swept his shells into the wastepaper bin. He gave the two juniors a grudging nod; praise for doing the job you were paid to do wasn't included in his old-school handbook.

"Any joy on your side, Carrie?" said Taylor. She handed the printouts back to Walker and eased back in her seat. Cook gave an eager nod and then tucked a flyaway strand of mousey hair behind her ear.

"Yes, actually," she said. "It seems Miss Jane Winifred Morrow is safe and sound and back in the arms of Jesus."

"It's a wonder he took her after the shenanigans she was up to."

Taylor waved Macpherson down and gestured for Cook to continue.

"When I got your text I contacted the admin department at Queen's University. The girl was really helpful and told me Jane Morrow transferred to the Ulster University Campus at Coleraine."

She tapped a few keys and read from her screen.

"Cited family issues and was able to shift and continue her studies closer to home. The family property is Ballymena, slap bang in the middle of the Bible belt. She gave me contact details and I spoke to her father. He's an evangelical pastor."

"One extreme to the other," said Macpherson.

"Shush your jaws a minute, will you," admonished Taylor. Cook continued.

"I got the sense he wasn't keen on her going to the big smoke in the first place so when she came back with her tail between her legs he was able to issue a bit of righteous admonishment."

"But she's okay?" said Taylor. Cook nodded.

"Oh yeah. She fell in with a bad boy and a badder crowd and she's been welcomed back into the arms of the Free Presbyterian community to repent her sins and atone for not listening to Daddy in the first place."

"So either Jane isn't the one haunting loopy Luna or she may hang up the crystals and get a real job," said Macpherson, his face a mask of faux shock.

"Actually, I did a bit more digging," said Cook, beckoning them over so she could share her screen.

"Teacher's pet," muttered Walker, eliciting a smirk from Macpherson.

"One year ago another student was reported missing in the same area after a night out. She had separated from friends and the last sighting of her was captured by CCTV as she crossed the Ormeau Bridge on her way home. Search and rescue were deployed to dredge the Lagan between there, the King's Bridge, and along the embankment but nothing was recovered. She's never been seen since."

"I vaguely remember that. We were working the Brookvale baseball bat murder at the time," said Taylor recalling events. "Apart from a missing girl, possibly drowned, what else have you?"

"Her name begins with a J. Josie Wyatt."

Macpherson blew out a breath. "You're reaching there, Carrie."

Cook started to protest.

"Doc's right," said Taylor. "If I take this to the DCI given it's based on a call from the local crank medium she'll laugh me out of the station."

Chris Walker was spluttering, the struggle to get his words out equal to his eagerness in searching through the pages of his printouts. Reilly beat him to the punch. She held out her phone.

"What about if you show her this?"

Taylor peered at the snapshot of a pendant on Reilly's phone. The DC flicked to the next picture showing engraved initials. Walker spread out a page on the desk showing the location of the find.

"We found it here." Walker prodded the contour lines. "At a recent dump site not a mile from where she went missing."

Taylor's phone rang before she could consider the coincidence further.

"DI Taylor?"

She listened, nodded, replaced the handset and then stood quickly.

"What is it?" said Macpherson.

"Luna Meehan has been assaulted in her home."

Chapter 6

LEIGH-ANNE ARNOLD gave a small wave as Taylor and Macpherson exited the Volvo.

It was too early in the evening for the covens of witches or warlocks to be touring Brunswick Street but just like the last time they had attended, parked cars narrowed the small street like an Ulster Fry narrowed the arteries. The situation was exacerbated by a rusting, yellow builders' skip abandoned half on, half off the kerb on the left-hand side.

"Is she okay?" said Taylor approaching along the pavement.

Arnold nodded, mumbling into her TETRA and receiving a clipped affirmative in return. The door to number seventy-four stood open behind her.

"She fine. Just shaken," she said.

"Does she know who it was?"

Arnold took a slow breath and stood aside as Macpherson trundled up behind Taylor.

"I think you better just go on in."

Macpherson's quizzical look was met with an eye-roll from

Arnold as he stepped into the house.

A draught swept up the short hallway and as they entered Luna's living space the eclectic order she had previously maintained was in disarray. The lamb skull lay broken on the hearth. Crystals, vessels and furnishings were strewn about, and the throws and cushions from the sofa lay scattered on the floor.

The lady of the house had rearranged the armchair by the bay window and was sat quietly nursing a glass. A footstool had been righted and on its surface sat the Ouija board.

"Are you okay?" said Taylor as she entered. The draught continued to cut through the room from the open kitchen door.

"It's not the first time. I'll be fine." Luna Meehan gave a stoic smile.

"Miss Meehan," said Macpherson. "Do you mind if I…?" he motioned towards the kitchen.

"Go ahead, sergeant. They're long gone."

Macpherson disappeared from view and Taylor took a knee beside the homeowner.

"Are you hurt?" she said, eyes searching for the physical signs of assault; abrasions, scratches, bruising.

"The damage is to the spirit not the flesh, inspector." Luna peered at her with rheumy eyes. "She needs us to find her."

"She?"

"The girl in the water."

Taylor took a breath and stood, she could hear Macpherson wrestling with the keys and the lock of the back door.

"What exactly happened here, Luna?" said Taylor.

"Her spirit came in the night. Restless. Raging. I woke and she was over the top of me; red eyes and wrapped in a burial shroud. When I couldn't quell her pain she lashed out." Luna gestured around the small room and to the door beyond. "She wanted her box back."

"Okay," said Taylor, steadying her voice and keeping her expression neutral. "I'm going to check on how my sergeant is getting on. Just give me a second."

Luna eased back in her armchair and took a short sip from her glass, then closed her eyes, her lips moving silently as if in prayer.

Macpherson was on the back step when Taylor entered.

"Did she see the wee bastard that did it?" he said.

The kitchen had been ransacked as violently as the living room. Cupboards were open, contents spilt out, and one door hung like a broken wing. In the middle of the floor was a pool of spoiling milk.

"It was the spirit of our missing girl," said Taylor, peering at the smashed glazing of the window. Large pieces of glass lay in the sink and on the countertop, with smaller shards and fragments littering the floor nearby.

Macpherson took a step down into the yard and beckoned Taylor forward.

"The only spirits here are the ones you tip down your throat."

On the rough concrete path leading to the entry sat a toughened plastic recycling box. It was filled with the empties of more than a dozen cheap gin and vodka bottles.

"I told you she was a crackpot from day one," he said.

"Maybe so," said Taylor, her gaze pausing on a patch of moss and mud under the window sill. "But I'll take a punt that neither our lady indoors nor the Lady of the Lagan wears a size ten work boot."

Macpherson followed her gaze to where a distinctive tread pattern and muddy smear marked the ground.

Chapter 7

THE DRIVE UP the coast had been pleasant for Reilly and Cook even though the thought of what lay at the end of the road was not.

It was a bright autumn day, the skies were clear, and sunlight dappled the windscreen as they travelled along the A2, first skirting the small town of Holywood and then, as they travelled a little further, past the signage and slip road leading to the Ulster Folk and Transport Museum and Ballycultra Townland. The museum's old buildings and dwellings had been preserved from across the island of Ireland and painstakingly rebuilt on the hundred and seventy-acre site.

Six miles later and with the dark smudge of Dumfries and Galloway visible against the glistening Irish Sea, Cook dabbed the brakes and eased the car off the dual carriageway and into the outskirts of the seaside commuter town of Bangor.

Their destination was a pretty chalet bungalow at the end of a short cul-de-sac. The property was rendered in pink pebbledash and surrounded by a white picket fence, the twisted stems of a magnolia bush threading through the slats.

A car was parked outside the house and as they got out the driver's door opened.

"DC Cook?"

"That's me, Chrissy is it?"

Chrissy Glover nodded, swapping handshakes with the two detectives.

"Thanks for arranging this," said Reilly. Glover waved a hand.

"No problem. I'll admit, it was a surprise to hear of a new development. I've been family liaison since Josie disappeared but obviously, time passes, the trail goes cold and you get new assignments."

Peter Wyatt was waiting at the open door as the visitors crunched up the gravel path.

"Hello, Peter," said Glover.

"Thanks for seeing us, Mister Wyatt," said Cook.

Wyatt gave a small nod and beckoned them in. He was late-forties, with red-blond hair and an oval face, and as Reilly followed him along a neat and tidy hallway she thought to herself that he bore a striking resemblance to the lead actor in a TV series but she couldn't place which.

Wendy Wyatt sat on a two-seater in a kitchen that opened into a sunroom. She was pretty but prematurely grey and had the haunted expression of someone living on their nerves.

A picture of her daughter sat on a nest of tables beside her.

"Have you found her?" she said. The tone of her voice was

calm but the whiteness of her knuckles gripping a tea towel betrayed her tension.

"I'm afraid not," said Cook before Glover extended introductions.

Wyatt offered them tea which they accepted along with a seat.

"We're following up on Josie's disappearance and have a few questions about how she was at the time, her friends, anything that might have seemed insignificant then but could help us now."

"We told Chrissy and the team everything," said Peter over the rumble of the kettle boiling in the background.

"Josie wouldn't run away," said Wendy. "She was a home bird. Something happened to her. Someone took her away."

"What's prompted this, detective." Peter Wyatt set down the cups and a plate of chocolate-covered oat-flake biscuits. His tone wasn't confrontational, but it was frank.

Cook shared a glance with Reilly. Glover spoke into the silence.

"The detectives are involved in another case which has turned up an item they would like you to look at."

Reilly took out a picture of the recovered pendant. Both sides of the charm and chain were set against a dark backdrop with forensic measurement markers framing the piece.

"Could you tell us if this belonged to Josie?" said Reilly.

The words were unnecessary, Wendy's reaction more explicit than anything she could have said. She snatched at the picture, tears in her eyes.

"Yes." Her voice was a hoarse whisper. She looked up at Peter who was also fighting back tears. The photograph was the first tangible link to their little girl in a year.

"She was wearing it the last time she was home. I teased her about it." Peter wiped his eyes, giving a terse laugh. "She's a Harry Potter nut. I think she liked it because it was witchy."

"How was she the last time she was home?" said Cook gently.

Peter blew out his cheeks and Wendy sniffed. Glover passed over a tissue and squeezed the mother's hand.

"Josie and I had a couple of days away. Just up the coast to Newcastle," said Wendy, blowing her nose, eyes fixed on the photo. "Her exams were coming up and she hadn't been home in a while. I wanted to spoil her before she started a new term."

"Was she in good spirits?" said Cook.

"She was in great form, although when I think back she could have been putting on a brave face."

"There had been a bit of stress over the exams," explained Peter. "And some angst over an admirer."

"Okay," said Cook with a nod. "Is that who gave her the necklace?"

"Possibly," Wendy shrugged. "She only ever referred to him as 'this fella' so I don't think she was taking any of it too seriously. Josie was always one for letting exam pressure build up so I know, for her, a relationship at that time was a no-go." Wendy gazed at the image. "She could have bought it herself. Peter's right; she loved those wizard books and she was never out of St George's Market."

Wendy gestured to a windowsill of photos that captured Josie's short life. Images from childhood through to teenager, the last was of a grinning young woman in striped scarf and witch's hat at a house party. Beside her beer bottles lined a countertop and ghostly white faces behind were blurred in the glare of a disco ball.

Clasped around her throat was the mirror and cat pendant.

Chapter 8

"...AND CHRISSY GLOVER confirms no boyfriend was ever traced during the initial inquiry," said Cook, summing up the trip to Bangor.

Taylor rubbed the knot forming between her eyebrows.

Somewhere in the background Michael Jackson's 'Thriller' was playing too loudly and there was a distracting bustle of activity as cleaners began to do the rounds and the shift change progressed, one lot eager to get off and begin a weekend of creepy celebrations and eerie activities, the other half bemoaning they would be missing out and would be left with the fall-out of the looney long weekend.

"What's your thoughts on the necklace turning up now?" said Macpherson.

"It's not it turning up now, it's the manner in which it did." Taylor rotated her shoulders. "We found Josie's pendant at a fly-tipping site. We now need to go back to the council and have the rubbish examined for any other personal items: clothes, shoes, underwear. I'll request help from the dog section and if they pick up any traces of cadaver amongst that…" She gave a grim twist of the lips. "Then it's the call to Seapark to get the SOCOs involved."

Each of them could see the investigation picking up pace and spiralling exponentially in cost and manpower.

"What we need to consider is, that by accident or design, someone used the illegal dumpers to get rid of evidence that's been missing for a year. Were they holding it as a trophy? Why the sudden need to get rid of it now, like this?"

"Are we anywhere closer to finding this white van?" said Macpherson to no one in particular.

Both Cook and Reilly replied with short shakes of heads.

"So we make it a priority to get a lead on that, however unlikely it is that the driver will be able to identify who gave him what to dump?" he added

"Not necessarily," said Taylor, standing and making her way to the board pinned with dump sites. "We know it was found here, near the boat club, and that section is impounded at Blackstaff council depot. So A, we identify any householders we haven't already from the rubbish and then run them through the system for previous form; history of violence, domestic abuse, the sex offenders register. Then B, when we find the driver we push him to recall details of that particular dump. How does he take the collection in, who loads the van, does he remember any wee details that might rip a few pages out of the book that we'll be throwing at him?"

Neither Macpherson nor the two DCs looked overly buoyed at their chances and Taylor knew it too; more than that she understood that an opportunist could have just added Josie's trinket to the pile.

"What else is there to do but start there?" she said.

"Guv?"

Taylor twisted away from the pinboard towards Chris Walker. The DC's face was red and he carried his jacket over his arm.

"Guv, I've got a witness for the night Josie went missing."

"Didn't I tell you it was worth keeping him?" said Macpherson with a clap. "Don't you listen to what these girls say about you, Chrissy boy, you're alright in my book."

"What have you got?" said Taylor.

"I visited campus and got speaking to a few tutors and classmates. The general consensus was that Josie was very bright but also very anxious about her upcoming exams,"

Macpherson rolled one hand over the other.

"Details, Christopher, get to the details." Walker sped up, words tripping out nineteen to the dozen.

"Josie was a regular at the McClay Library. She spent hours in there and one member of staff knew her well enough to talk to. The girl's called Hannah Crawford. Anyway, Hannah had a boyfriend who also did Chinese deliveries for a restaurant at the time of the disappearance."

"While I've still got all my own teeth will you get to the point, fella?" snapped Macpherson.

"Hannah's boyfriend had picked her up that night when she got off and they saw Josie and an IC1 male walking together in the direction of the Holylands."

"Did she have a name?" said Taylor. Walker nodded.

"The social scene is pretty incestuous so she did recognise him from a house party. I got an address too."

"We got there in the end," said Macpherson with a sigh. He stood, crooking a finger at the DC's notebook. "Give us a look. You've either got the last person to see the wee girl alive or the mystery boyfriend; or for a bonus point, both."

"Here you go," said Walker.

"Ack in the name of God, are you serious?"

Macpherson handed the notebook, containing the neatly printed address, to Taylor.

"When you said you'd be back I didn't think you meant so soon."

"Can we come in, Max?" said Taylor.

Max Parker deliberated for half a second and then turned and walked up the hallway, leaving them to follow.

"Another wee soirée planned, eh?" said Macpherson.

The devastation of eighty-eight Cairo Street had been repaired to a degree. The lounge was rubbish free and the kitchenette tidied. A selection of beer and wine was on the floor and Parker bent down to lift a twenty-four pack of cider and set it out on the back step.

When he turned back he gave a shrug.

"Halloween isn't it."

"But you don't need that as an excuse to party, son."

Parker chuckled. "No, I suppose not." He eased up against the worktop. "If you've more questions about Jane I've nothing else to tell you."

"We're not here about Jane," said Taylor; neither detective had made a motion to sit.

"So?" Parker drew out the question. "What can I help you with?"

"Did you know Josie Wyatt?"

Parker was quick, but not quick enough to hide the recognition.

"Not really," he said at length.

"But she was here." Taylor gestured around the space. "Parties, social get-togethers, whatever?"

"She might have been once or twice."

"What did you think when she went missing?"

"I don't know. That it was terrible?"

"You asking or telling, son?" said Macpherson.

"It was terrible. No one wants to hear of something bad happening to somebody they know."

"Something bad?" said Taylor. Parker pulled a face, shrugged and raised his hands.

"Going missing. Snatched. Fell in the Lagan drunk and drowned. Whatever happened that night?"

"But other than what was reported, you've no idea of what might have transpired that night?"

"None," said Parker empathically.

"Did you and her ever…" Macpherson let the query hang.

"No."

"What about your housemate? David, isn't it?" said Taylor.

"Davy?" Parker huffed out a laugh. "Davy's not that way inclined I don't think."

"You don't think?" said Macpherson.

"I've never known him to bring anybody back after a night out, never mind any girls," said Parker.

"Maybe he's just paranoid they'd fall for your charms," said Taylor. A small cock of the head as she saw she had struck a nerve.

"He's your mate but I'm pretty sure I know where your priorities lie, Max. You'd sell your granny for a quick tussle between the sheets and it wouldn't matter who you stepped on." She turned, lifting a picture off the mantlepiece. It showed a raucous crowd of young men in a club, arms around each other. On the periphery, almost in the background was David Black.

"Josie's parents say she had a boyfriend."

"Well, it wasn't me." Parker took a step forward. "What is this? First Jane and now Josie? Are you trying to fit me up?"

"Do you recognise this?"

Taylor pulled a picture of the mirror pendant from her pocket. Parker took a quick look.

"No."

She nodded, seemingly satisfied with his answer.

"You're sure?"

"I'm sure," said Parker.

"Could we ask David?"

"Davy?" Parker's tone was incredulous.

"We've had a witness come forward who saw David and Josie walking near here the night she went missing. We just need to establish where they parted ways. If he noticed anybody suspicious in the area? Does he remember her wearing that necklace?"

"Davy?"

"Yes. Is he here?" Taylor's voice was clipped and seemed to jolt Parker out of his thoughts.

"He's at work still."

"When's he usually home?"

"There's a few of us going for drinks at the Rugby Club. Davy was meeting us there and giving lifts back for the party," explained Parker.

Taylor nodded at the crest on his tee shirt.

"Sports Association Club near the Lockview?"

"Aye."

Taylor knew the spot. Manicured sports pitches, a clubhouse and bar sat on open ground on the edge of the forest park. The Lagan towpath ran along the fringe to Lockview, a tourist lookout point where the River Lagan swelled before channelling into the deep vicious bend at The Devil's Elbow.

"Okay, Max. Thanks." She put down the photo, noticing her card still on the mantle. She tapped it.

"Tell Davy it's in his best interests to call and not to have me come look for him."

Parker nodded mutely and Taylor gestured for Macpherson to lead the way out. Parker flipped the hall light switch as they made their way towards the front door.

Taylor stopped.

"Are these yours, Max?"

Parker followed her finger to a pair of work boots nudged under a radiator cover. She stooped to peer at the soles and the scummy residue smeared on the leather upper.

"Are you hard of hearing, son?" growled Macpherson.

Taylor, having pulled a latex glove from her inside jacket pocket had carefully lifted one boot, examining the sole to find mud and moss mashed into the tread. Near the heel were several chunks of glass.

"Max?" she said again. Parker blinked twice before he answered.

"They're Davy's."

Chapter 9

"SAY AGAIN, ERIN?"

Reilly's voice had cut out as she shifted the call to hands-free.

"A white Renault Kangoo. Registration matches the partial we received," she repeated much more clearly.

"Okay, great. We're about five minutes from the sports grounds," said Taylor.

She gripped the overdoor handle as Macpherson thundered the Volvo along Stranmillis Embankment heading for Lockview and the sportsplex. Her phone was connected to Bluetooth so Macpherson could listen in.

"What about the connection to Josie?" she said.

The three DCs were gathered around a conference phone back at Musgrave Street. Taylor had informed them of developments at Cairo Street and requested uniformed back-up to the house, both to keep an eye on Parker and in the event she missed Black at the clubhouse. His boots were bagged and would be analysed against the soil and glass samples from Luna Meehan's house.

Parker, having discovered a long-overdue sense of loyalty to his housemate found his resistance crushed under Macpherson's blunt persuasion, the DS intimating that the lack of assistance was tantamount to the aiding and abetting of an offender. Adequately subdued, Parker guided them up to David Black's room.

Careful that she wasn't about to jeopardise a potential future case, Taylor had a look inside, the snoop yielding little other than Black's taste in music which leaned towards gothic and alternative rock, a selection of art prints by H.R. Giger, and a shelf of sci-fi fantasy literature.

Walker's voice came on the line with Cook accessing the central database and putting the documents relating to Wyatt's disappearance up on a display screen.

"David Black was routinely questioned along with others who were with Josie on the night she went missing. All interviewees say she left the bar early on her own. No reason why. There was no mention of Black or anyone else leaving to walk her home and they all alibied each other for the duration of the night afterwards."

"Doesn't mean to say Black or anyone else didn't slip out unnoticed," said Reilly, her voice losing clarity as the Volvo passed through a spotty patch of coverage.

"Chris, speak again to the girl in the library and narrow down a timeframe of when she saw Josie and Black together. We can press Parker and revisit the other statements if she can give us a window to work in," said Taylor. Macpherson slowed the car as the sports pitches loomed ahead under floodlights.

"Guv," Walker confirmed his instruction.

"And Carrie, check ANPR in and around any of the sites of the fly-tipping and see if we can't pick up Black's vehicle now we know what we're looking for. Actually, extend that to yesterday evening in the vicinity of Brunswick Road too. We're here," said Taylor. "I'll check in with you again shortly."

She closed the call as Macpherson bumped the Volvo down a rutted lane in desperate need of resurfacing. To the left and protected by a row of stakes and a low chain were the pitches. Several scattered groups were involved in drills or practice matches which even the thud of the Volvo's sump tank striking the lip of a deep pothole didn't distract from.

The right-hand side was rough gravel car parking, skirted by a barriered walkway leading up to the squat clubhouse and changing facilities. Signage pointed to the various pitches and towards the track that ran into the wooded area behind the buildings and onto the Lagan towpath beyond.

Macpherson pulled up, the two detectives seeking out a white Renault Kangoo van in the collection of cars and other vehicles.

"There," said Taylor. A white van sat on its own at the end of a row of spaces. Macpherson nudged the Volvo into gear.

As they approached from the passenger side their headlights swept across the bodywork, a ghostly swooping pattern and the remnants of a phone number were visible where exposure had burned the images of old decals into the side panel.

Macpherson pulled up behind. Close enough to make exiting the space difficult. A quick visual scan confirmed the plates matched the partials.

The van's interior light illuminated as a figure emerged. Male, dark haired, rangy and dressed in working clothes. He made to pull the back door open, then squinted into the glare.

Taylor stepped out.

"David Black?"

Black let go of the door handle and ran.

"....suspect is on foot travelling in the direction of Lockview and the Lagan towpath. Officer in pursuit."

Macpherson wrestled the TETRA handset from its charging unit on the console, and ducked back out of the car, looking east.

Black led Taylor by a good fifty yards, his arms pumping furiously as he sprinted in a straight line for the gloom of the pines.

"Why couldn't the wee bastard have just stood apiece?" he grumbled to himself, wrenching open the rear door of the Kangoo.

He slammed it home almost instantly and blew out a disgusted breath.

The stink of decomposing food waste, fuel and rot was overwhelming. The single glimpse he had managed had shown an interior packed with plastic bin liners and loose household waste material.

"Right, you wee shite, you're for the high jump when I get

my hands on you for making me run."

Macpherson wrangled the earpiece of the radio into position and joined the chase.

Chapter 10

THE PATH WAS treacherous.

Underfoot, the gravel track which had skirted the sportsplex car park had transitioned into the towpath, the surface soaked as rainwater ran off the higher ground and down a winding slope and steps cut into the bank leading to the Lagan walkway. The path was covered in a carpet of perilous, slimy leaves and Taylor lashed out a hand to steady herself from slipping.

Out of sight, but not too far distant she heard Black curse as he stumbled, losing the delicate balance of speed over safety.

The harsh barks of competition and training still echoed from the pitches, but each ragged lungful of air and the banks of foliage passing with every stride deadened the shouts.

Taylor slipped and slid the last few feet onto the hard-packed towpath, two feet of grass and bullrushes separating her from the black surface of the Lagan's waters.

The gloom was sudden and complete. The glare of the pitchside floodlights continued to blink through the swaying branches of the treetops but did nothing to illuminate the path.

She could see Black ahead, a strip of luminous material on his work jacket marking him out as he fled, heading for a small iron and wood bridge that crossed the narrow end of the big pool beside the tourist lookout of Lockview. The small coffee shop and tourist information office was closed and offered no light to guide hunter or prey.

The building sound of rushing water took over from its lazy lap against the banks of soft vegetation as Taylor made the footbridge in time to see Black step off the other side and descend the path towards The Devil's Elbow.

The route zigzagged through the tree line alongside the narrow channel where the calm flowing water was suddenly forced down and funnelled into a deep gully that cut ninety degrees through a V of limestone.

"Ronnie!"

Taylor turned to see a wobbling beam of torchlight mark out Macpherson as he made the towpath behind her. She looked back, seeking Black's shadow moving through the gaps of the trees but not finding him. She took a deep breath and plunged down the slope in pursuit.

The rest of Macpherson's shouts were drowned out by the surge of water.

"Don't boke. Don't boke. Don't boke."

Macpherson chanted the mantra as he pushed the sensation of vomiting down and urged himself forward. After half a mile racing to catch up, his short arms and legs were moving like misaligned pistons.

"Ronnie!" The shout was more a gasp as he threaded his way across the narrow footbridge, the roar and motion of the water rushing underneath disorienting as he peered down past his rubber legs and between the planks.

Reaching the far side, he paused, heaving in breaths and aiming the torch beam towards the slope of The Devil's Elbow.

The first few passes caught nothing, and then he saw her.

His partner had reached the end of a switchback and had paused to either catch her breath or reorientate on the fleeing David Black.

Macpherson took another shuddering breath and started to move, his guts freezing as the torch beam bounced through the branches to catch movement rushing in from her blind side.

"Ronnie!" he screamed.

Taylor never heard the warning over the roar of the water but she felt the sudden impact.

For several seconds she hung suspended in thin air, then suddenly her stomach flipped, a wash of spray misted her face and she plunged into the icy water.

Her immersion was sudden and terrifying.

The rage of the water flipped her over and her head struck a rock but before she had time to register the impact, the torrent whipped her away.

Shock and the freezing water held the pain at bay but its grip dragged her deeper into the darkness.

Taylor flailed, hands desperately searching for a way to arrest her momentum but her fingers found nothing but slimy rocks and tree roots. The cold and the constant flipping around was disorientating and, kicking wildly, she sought the surface, her lungs screaming for oxygen but unable to tell which way was up or down.

Finally, her head broke through and she gulped a half breath of air and a mouthful of water. Choking up the latter and caught in a fit of coughing she battled the eddies, vainly sculling for the edge but only finding sheer sandstone, earning another bruising battering as she careered against the rocks to then be thrust back into the surge.

The roar was deafening and her limbs were losing feeling and mobility as the cold sucked the life from them, her central nervous system battling to redirect heat to her core at the expense of her extremities.

Another rock slipped past, another overhanging branch remained tantalisingly out of reach and then she caught hold of a jagged crevice.

Taylor felt her shoulder scream as the force of the water tried to break her grip, the torrent hauling her deeper into the churning depths of The Devil's Elbow. She howled in anger and frustration, reaching her free hand around to assist her tenuous hold and earning another lungful of water in the process.

Two feet away, rising like a spectre from the bubbling water, the pale face of David Black broke the surface. His face was set in a grimace as he barrelled into her.

Taylor's fingers broke free and the two were dragged under the water.

"Code Zero. Code Zero. Officer in need of assistance. Devil's Elbow at Lockview. Officer in the water."

Macpherson's breath came in shallow, panting gasps as he made his report on the hoof. Continuing his slip, slide, shuffle along the rutted path he began to consider that with the throbbing in his head and the crushing band beginning to encircle his chest, if he didn't quit the running soon he'd be needing an ambulance of his own.

David Black had rushed from cover amongst the trees to shove Taylor off the path and into the raging river. Unfortunately for Black and to Macpherson's surprise, the suspect lost his footing as he pivoted away, toppling sideways to bounce down the steep rocky bank into the water.

Macpherson searched the raging current tearing through the deep narrow canyon of The Devil's Elbow. The torch beam danced back and forth to no avail. There was no sign of either Taylor or Black.

The TETRA warbled and he pressed his earpiece, struggling to separate the violence of the rapids from the confirmation units had been despatched for assistance.

"Ronnie!" he shouted.

Taylor's head broke the surface, her mouth open, gasping for air as the malevolent figure of Black clambered over her seeking buoyancy.

Both disappeared below the black surface once more,

Macpherson's torch beam left dancing impotent circles on the waves.

Black's hands were wrapped around her throat, and Taylor grunted as his knees dug into her back as he kicked and thrashed.

All the while she held her breath, biting on her lip to keep the impact of his feet scrambling up her shins and thighs from knocking out the last of the valuable oxygen the fight was using up much too quickly.

They spun and twisted in the violence of the rapids, each strike of rock and root trying but failing to split them apart or stop their freefall through the deep-water canyon, the impact on occasion causing more sunken vegetation to join them in the swollen cascade charging downstream.

Taylor gouged at Black, her fingers seeking the soft tissue around his eyes and mouth, scratching and writhing to gain some kind of purchase.

Black, although willowy, held on with a vice-like grip and with the pressure on her larynx tightening, Taylor convulsed. She coughed, immediately inhaling but the reflex only serving to let more water in.

The gloom of the water darkened as her grip loosened, the battle against hypoxia lost.

She had never really considered dying in the line of duty. If she had, she doubted it would have been drowning that offered the fateful way out. Shot or stabbed probably; blown up like her father? Less likely now, but you could never rule it out.

The cold of the water began to fade, a feeling of near euphoria slowly seeped up from the nape of her neck and her vision prickled with flecks of light.

Something touched her hand and instinctively she grabbed it for buoyancy, but the cascade crashed them once again against the rocks. Black released his grip, his feet kicking her deeper into the dark.

Taylor was limp. Lifeless.

Her hand gripped what felt like a thin branch flowing alongside, and she focused the last of her consciousness on the touch.

Her thoughts were with Macpherson on the riverbank, of the pain she knew he would endure at her loss but also of the contentment she would feel at re-joining the parents so cruelly snatched away in her youth. Would they be proud? Would they be glad to see her?

The branch was wrapped in flimsy sacking and as Taylor gripped it tighter she let herself ride the currents, suddenly propelled upwards and out of the whirling depths.

Breaking the surface she voided her lungs and stomach of brackish water, thrashing at the loose material that was coiling around her limbs.

The branch, she realised was an arm and thinking it was Black, she recoiled, but the face she looked into was serene.

David Black gagged as he broke the surface of the raging water, spewing what felt like a gallon of the Lagan mixed with bitter bile. Each effort was more tiring than the last, and now he had lost the slight advantage he had held by using the woman for buoyancy, he felt weaker.

Cold, alone, and at the mercy of The Devil's Elbow, he suddenly felt a stab of guilt and regret at the situation he was in.

On the right-hand bank, a beam of torchlight flitted across the water. Indecipherable shouts carried across the night; calls that he knew weren't out of concern for him.

A sudden clarity descended as he continued to be buffeted around in the water. Long lost sermons from a restrictive childhood reverberating around inside his head, coupled with images of a sour-faced man with skin the pallor of death and nicotine breath. His message: Be sure your sins will find you out.

As the years passed David had come to realise his sins were not those of the flesh but of silence. A silence that had enabled the preacher to continue his reign of abuse until cancer delivered the long-overdue judgement.

He hadn't meant for it to happen. He hadn't woken that day and thought to murder, but when she laughed in his face all the pent up feelings of shame and defilement, of rejection and rage, bottled up over the course of his life, erupted in violence.

Who was she to speak to him like that, to judge him? Why had the preacher singled him out? Why was it fair that the Neanderthals like Parker and the others could tempt women to their beds as easily as fruit falling from the forbidden tree.

Black's hands twisted into fists, he smashed them impotently into the water as flashbacks of Josie Wyatt's last night coursed through his mind. Her struggle, the unexpected weight of her body as he shoved it into the van, the exertion of wrapping her in old sheets and then the welcome release as he dumped her off the bridge into the very waters that were now trying to drag him to his fate and a reckoning of his own.

A metre away the police officer surfaced, vomiting and thrashing. She was caught in some of the industrial detritus that found its way into the river, struggling to free herself from the pale sacking that was sucking her back under.

Black was buffeted away, salvation appearing in the form of a broken tree and the fork of fallen branch which dipped into the water. He stretched out a hand, the thick trunk holding as he pulled with the last of his strength against the surging waters. Struggling to drag his head from the bow wave created as the torrent swept against his body, he saw the woman break free from her binding, the material caught in the maelstrom swirled away at speed.

Black hooked his arm under the branch and caught his breath, exhaustion and the cold as dangerous now as when he had battled the current.

He watched the police officer swoosh past but made no attempt to reach out, her face was peaceful, her expression resigned.

Shifting to secure his grip, he looked back upstream. A shudder tore through him as he realised what he was looking at and then he gave an involuntary cry as the ghoul rose from the water.

He let go of the branch and at once he was snatched up by the water, but not fast enough to avoid the clutches of the horror that embraced him.

Black's blood-curdling screams echoed over the roar of the water as he stared into the face of Josie Wyatt.

Her lips were pulled back in a grimace of decomposition and the patches of hair that remained stuck to what was left of her scalp were thin and lank.

Sightless sockets glared in accusation as Black battled to free himself from her thin arms; limbs that, although they were more bone than flesh, now held greater strength than in life as they pulled him under the water to face judgement.

Epilogue

Macpherson pulled up the collar of his raincoat to ward off the wind sweeping across the exposed cemetery. The patter of rain beat a gentle tattoo on the canopy of his umbrella to accompany the solemnity of the coffin lowering.

His gaze lingered on the weeping relatives for a few more seconds before searching downhill beyond the rows of granite headstones to a plot shaded by a pale golden canopy of silver birch trees.

While it could be classed as uncommon, it wasn't without precedent for victim and violator to find themselves interred in the same consecrated ground.

David Black lay far enough away to be out of sight, and as Macpherson watched the rooks begin to roost in the thin branches of the treetops, he knew from grim experience that his crimes would never be far from the minds of those now living with the consequences.

For Peter and Wendy Wyatt, while the return of their

daughter was not in the manner they had hoped, they were grateful to have a body to bury and a place to finally mourn. Even if they did have to share it with her killer.

"Are you alright?" he said to the person sheltering under the cover of his umbrella, squeezing the arm entwined through his own.

Taylor nodded. The scabs on her face were healing but still told a story of a narrow escape.

"I'm fine," she said. And she was, now, but it had been a rough couple of days directly afterwards.

Pulled by Macpherson from the calmer waters at the mouth of The Devil's Elbow it had taken uniform and the paramedics time to negotiate the path to the riverbank and by that time hypothermia had set in. Rushing her to the Ulster Hospital for treatment, it had taken doctors the first two days to gradually warm her and even two weeks later she was still more susceptible to the cold, but the worst of the injuries that remained were cuts and bruises.

Not that it was just the physical preventing her return to work. Her mental health required assessment and sign-off and it would be another week before she returned to duty and only after a referral to occupational health had been agreed with time scheduled to talk and come to terms with her experiences under the eye of a service professional.

She still hadn't spoken to anyone about the minutes where she believed she would die, nor the vision of Josie Wyatt.

"Damn thing, eh," said Macpherson into the keen of the wind.

No one had as yet been able to explain what exactly had occurred, other than speculate that their plunge and desperate wash through the rapids had somehow dislodged the previously sunken body of Wyatt.

"Two birds with one stone," said Taylor.

After the initial frantic commotion to rescue Taylor and get her to hospital, attention had turned to Black's van which had contained another consignment of illegal waste. Working to the adage that where there was muck there was brass, Black had begun private waste collection as a side hustle to his job with the council, his endeavour hitting the skids when a new manager reprimanded him for skirting regulations and permit controls by bringing van loads of rubbish to landfill, and for not having a waste carrier's licence. With his initial plans foiled it left him looking at the back alleys, quiet beauty spots and the side roads of the city to offload.

A follow-up search of Cairo Street produced Josie Wyatt's handbag and some of her jewellery, the evidence damning Black when coupled with Hannah Crawford's now official statement naming him as the last person to be seen with the victim.

Taylor shifted her weight to ease the pain in her back which still hadn't fully recovered from her rollercoaster descent through The Devil's Elbow. In the end, she guessed, it was a tale as old as crime itself. Spurned love. Rage over rejection. A crime of passion.

The service was wrapping up with handshakes and hugs.

"It's good to see you looking better, inspector."

Taylor released Macpherson's arm and they both turned to face the voice.

Luna Meehan had left the pointed hat and broomstick at Brunswick Street but still managed to maintain an air of witchery.

"I've been reading in the newspapers about what happened," she said.

Macpherson scoffed and gave a shake of the head.

"Sure you know reading that twaddle only encourages them to write more," he grunted.

"Are you keeping okay yourself, after everything?" said Taylor.

Luna smiled, raising her chin to point down the hill towards the unseen mound of mud and flowers that marked Black's grave.

"The dead will do you no harm, it's the living you need to watch out for."

"Isn't that the truth." Macpherson gestured back towards the car park and the shelter and dodgy heaters of the Volvo. "Ronnie?"

"Actually, inspector, I hoped you would do me a favour before you get off?" said Luna.

"Christ, this better not be another one of your ghost hunts?"

"Away and get the car," said Taylor, laying a placating hand on his arm.

Macpherson gave the medium an arch look. "I'm fine," said Taylor.

He nodded, handing over the umbrella and then trundling off up the hill with a limp, not quite fully recovered from his own exertions.

"He's a character," said Luna.

"He is that." Taylor smiled as she watched the man who had stepped into her parents' shoes walk away, his lips moving in a silent grumble.

"What can I do for you?"

Luna reached into her large shoulder bag and pulled out the charity shop trinket box.

"I wondered if you could give it back to her parents?"

"Luna, we don't even know if—"

"It's hers," said the medium.

Taylor nodded, taking the box and not wanting to make a scene. Conscious of what had happened in the river, she paused, thinking of a way she could frame her question and understand her belief it was Josie Wyatt who had guided her to safety.

"Coincidence is just the dead leaving us breadcrumbs, inspector," said Luna. "I believe we go on existing in this place after we've gone. That maybe we have more to do when unburdened of the physical." She paused, looking to the funeral party. "To those like me that brings comfort, but I understand others need more tactile memories."

"I'll give it to them," said Taylor.

"Thank you, inspector. I'm glad you're okay."

Taylor smiled her thanks and shook the woman's hand, turning then to walk down the narrow path between the headstones to intercept the Wyatts.

Luna Meehan watched her go, then nodded a greeting to a couple paying their respects under the shade of an ancient elm. They were about the same age as the Wyatts and their gaze followed the young detective inspector as she wound her way down the path.

Luna Meehan smiled and stepped onto the grass to walk amongst the dead.

Sometimes parents lost their daughters, and sometimes daughters lost their parents but death was no more the end of love than the horizon was the end of the earth.

When she glanced back the couple was gone.

Afterword

THANK-YOU FOR READING 'THE DEVIL'S ELBOW'

I sincerely hope you enjoyed this short story. If you can **please** spare a moment to leave a short review it will be very much appreciated and helps immensely in assisting others to find this, and my other books.
Follow Detective Inspector Veronica Taylor and her team in my Debut novel:

'CODE OF SILENCE'

Read on to get an EXCERPT or catch up with more of the BELFAST CRIME CASE-FILES in:

'BEHIND CLOSED DOORS'
'INTO THIN AIR'

You can find out about this book and more in the series by signing up at my website:

www.pwjordanauthor.com

CODE OF SILENCE: AN EXTRACT

Chapter 1

"…REPORTS OF A shooting in East Belfast earlier this evening. There are limited details at the minute, but the PSNI have cordoned off Risky's Nightclub. Initial accounts of the incident suggest one dead and one seriously injured. We'll update the information as it comes in…"

Tyres squealed in the semi-darkness, echoing off bare and scored concrete walls as the lone vehicle descended into the underground garage. Overhead strip lighting which strobed across the darkened windshield of the Vauxhall pool car was overwhelmed by the mute blue flash of the internal strobe light.

"…narrowly averting tragedy in a horrific collision and car fire following a high-speed pursuit in the city centre. The unnamed police officer has been hailed for their quick and selfless actions in rescuing a woman and her child trapped in the burning wreckage. A forty-one-year-old man has been arrested. Sources at the scene report that…"

"…from Section Eight had the scene under control and signed me off… Thank you, sir. I appreciate that. I'm just glad they were okay."

The Vauxhall bottomed out as it descended into the lower parking area, a crash and grind of undercarriage sending sparks dancing under the chassis.

"I'm pulling into the car park now. Yes, Chief Inspector. Nothing on a motive for this one as yet and no one has stepped up to claim it… No. We have a witness being treated at the scene and they'll be brought to the Royal once deemed fit for travel. I'll do an initial interview there asap… Sir, I can assure you none of that will influence my investigation and I'll keep the DCI up to speed… No problem. Night, sir."

The car pulled in with a final screech of rubber on wet painted concrete and the whine of the electronic handbrake. The driver's door clunked open, the ping of a warning tone emitting from the dashboard, the engine ticking over as it cooled.

"Evening, boss."

Detective Inspector Veronica 'Ronnie' Taylor eased out of the driver's seat, bleary-eyed, a pen clamped between her teeth, and juggling an iPhone, car keys, parking ticket and a handful of loose change.

"Hi, Doc. Sorry, I got here as quick as I could," Taylor mumbled through gritted teeth, offering a handshake.

"No bother. It's not like our boys got anywhere else to be. Good job up the road."

Detective Sergeant Doc Macpherson had the grip of a bear with a bone and the paws to match. Which was odd considering his moniker derived from his uncanny likeness to one of Snow White's famous friends. He reached past her, noticing body armour strewn on the back parcel shelf, a crumpled set of clothes stuffed in a Tesco bag for life in the footwell, and the stink of burning plastic. He shoved the door closed with a solid thump.

Taylor jangled the keys and change into her pockets and checked the screen of her phone. Missed calls and notifications. It followed the keys and change into the depths of her smart but wrinkled jacket. She pulled out a small tin of Clove Rock.

"Cheers. Here, I brought you a present."

"You shouldn't have." Macpherson accepted the token with a wide grin and clicked them open, offering her the first, which she accepted.

"ME here and all?"

"I think the creepy bugger hangs upside down in one of those lockers, to be honest."

Taylor delivered a tired but conspiratorial smile. She swept her chestnut hair up into a high messy bun and secured it with the pen. The movement releasing Eau de Burning Car Wreck into the surrounding air. She brushed a loose lock from her eyes.

"Who's holding the scene at the club?"

"Walker is SLO. He'll be fine," the DS assured her, noticing the sudden uptick of her chin at the mention of the new detective constable. "SOCOs are still there and half the night shift have the place cordoned off, but the punters are up for a riot. MSU are on standby to deploy and break it up. Reilly is accompanying the witness as soon as the paramedics give a fit to travel."

Taylor nodded, confirming she had received that brief.

Macpherson glanced at his watch.

"Last ETA one hour. We need to hold off until the doctor confirms capacity and consent."

Taylor raised an eyebrow in query.

"If this is who we think, we need to tick the boxes and make sure any testimony we get is solid."

"If it gets us our way back into the Firm, maybe I'll not end up in uniform after all," said Taylor.

Macpherson grunted and gestured to the nearby doors with their innocuous but ominous blue printed signage.

"We'll know soon enough. Don't be getting ahead of yourself. For one, this character's not in the position to be offering Queen's Evidence any time soon. After you."

Veronica Taylor blipped the Vauxhall's locks and led the way towards the underground entrance to the Royal Belfast Hospital Regional Forensic Mortuary.

The morgue wasn't a place that held a lot of fond memories for Taylor. Fragments of pain. Personal and professional. She had lost count of the times she'd stood in sombre vigil as a loved one identified a body, not that it was ever just a body.

Their footfalls clipped along terrazzo-effect linoleum until they were buzzed through into reception and received by a distracted middle-aged woman in washed-out green scrubs. She glanced up then returned to typing, the loud clackety-clack of keys under stubby red-tipped and chipped fingernails audible under her mutterings.

"Evening, he's expecting you. You can go on through. Sorry, we've another due for collection by the undertakers and someone who was in a rush to leave for the weekend misplaced the notes," she explained without looking up; a dark line between arched brows as she frowned at the screen then the clackety-clack as she remedied an error.

Like any normal establishment at half ten on a Sunday night, there was a quiet and stillness that preceded the flip into a new week and the madness of a Monday morning. As they walked the short distance along the eerie corridor, Macpherson, in anticipation, broke out the clove sweets. Popping one in his mouth he offered another to Taylor. Arriving at a familiar stainless steel door, frosted windows hiding the sights within, the sergeant, with a nod of deference, offered his colleague the first step over the threshold.

The sterile and clinical smell of the cutting room met them before the glass doors had fully swept closed. Tonight there was also a numb silence. No howl of dissection saw and no roar of the high-powered overhead ventilation sucking out the stench of decomposition and ruptured bowel. The faint odour of raw meat however refused to be overpowered by the scent of harsh disinfectant wafting from the plugholes of the stainless steel sinks that lined the rear wall. Glass-fronted cabinets above revealed instruments of horror that Taylor wished she had never seen used. The suite's once white tiles were now looking a little tired after years of soaking up spilt blood and gore. The centrepiece of the room was the four ominous steel tables atop one of which resided a formless mass hidden under a white sheet. Scales hung on meat hooks overhead, yet to be filled with human offal.

"Thanks for coming in, Professor Thompson."

"Never off duty, Inspector. Always hanging around here. You know what it's like in this caper."

Taylor ignored the splutter and flushed chubby red cheeks as Macpherson stifled his guffaw under a hasty cough, pantomime slapping his chest.

"Let it not be said I am one to let a lady down in her hour of need." Thompson gave her a theatrical bow, and a concerned look to the scarlet faced DS.

"You ought to give up the smokes, Sergeant or Irene will be writing up your certificate."

"Sorry, Prof. Choked on a sweetie there," said Macpherson, clearing his throat but grinning and shaking the man's hand.

The pathologist then offered his hand to Taylor, grip a lot more social than her sergeant's who had busied himself with searching out two disposable aprons and face-masks.

"Apparently, there's been a bit of a mix-up and Irene isn't a happy bunny. One of those weeks ahead, I fear. Shall we?" Thompson passed across a manila file containing the still-warm printouts the inspector had requested on the phone on her way in. Taylor opened and skim-read the details, taking in a few of the close-up facial pictures of the victim and the broad overview shots of the scene. Thompson, whilst scrubbing up, filled the two detectives in on what details he had; male, late forties, one hundred and eighty-five centimetres tall, weight eighty-seven kilos. Thompson's mortuary assistant loaded a tray with surgical instruments: scissors, rib shears, plastic tubes and hoses. The collection was then deposited into what was essentially an industrial dishwasher for sterilisation before the autopsy. As the assistant unscrewed the blade of a large surgical scalpel Thompson finished washing and gowning and then with help from Macpherson he snapped on a pair of latex gloves.

"Voila!"

The pathologist whipped back the white sheet with a flourish that a Parisian maître d' would have been proud of.

The photographs didn't do him justice. The corpse stared at the ceiling. He had died hard.

Drum and bass. Vibrations that outside began as a tinny bmm-tsk, bmm-tsk, bmm-tsk now thrummed underfoot and rose in tremulous waves that pounded through the organs and threatened to loosen fillings from their moorings. Heavy footfalls were masked by the music, yet somehow the knock was heard and the door to the inner sanctum opened.

A pair of eyes bulged from tear-stained sockets. Desperate for salvation.

Murder could never be easy. Quick perhaps, but never easy. A life ripped violently apart and not just in the physical sense. At a point, there was a sudden visceral realisation that all that had ever been and all that had yet to be was gone.

In the door's opening, she knew what was happening. Knew her time had come. Another scream ripped from blood-spattered lips, the sound obscured by the binding of cloth duct tape. She felt a broken rib snag sending shockwaves of excruciating pain through her body.

"Good job, Gary. You can fuck off now, love. Tell Raymond drinks are on the house for you tonight," said the newcomer.

"Ah, okay. Right enough, Mr Millar. Cheers now." Gary wiped the back of his hand across a sweaty and blood-dappled forehead, his breath laboured.

Millar patted him as he passed, hand lingering a little too long on the younger man's bicep. The cheap Umbro tee shirt stuck to him, a wide inverted arch of sweat staining darker from throat to midsection.

"Now you know our arrangement, Gary. Not a word and maybe I'll call you in again for another wee job. Sound good?"

"Oh, aye. No bother, not a peep." Gary nodded. His eyes flashed back on his handiwork, then to Millar's hand on his arm. The sickening twist of guilt overridden by another craving.

"Erm, and my other gear?"

"In the back room with Rowdy. Don't be greedy and shoot it all up in one sitting now, will you?"

"No. No. Thanks again. I appreciate it."

Millar patted the boy on both his sweaty acne-scarred cheeks, his words warm, the tone cold, and his eyes devoid of emotion.

"No, Gary. Thank you."

Millar dragged the only other chair from the corner and across the bare floor, wooden legs scoring lurid marks as it skittered over the gaps between the floorboards. The space was illuminated by a single bare sixty-watt bulb dangling from a broken ceiling rose. Damp and mildew hung in the air. Detritus littered a space that had been commandeered as storage. Old plastic beer crates were haphazardly stacked and broken bottles lined a wall. Retired sound equipment, an old metal catering table, pitted and scratched with use, and a bowed rail of lost coats stood over an old, ruptured leather sofa. Discarded wraps of foil and the odd used condom wrapper were trapped in the seat cushions; the bouncers using it as a perk if they pulled a drunken clubber. Questions of consent closed with cold threats of something worse.

Placing the chair in front of his prisoner, Millar sat, one leg thrown over the other. He retrieved a pack of cigarettes from the inside pocket of his immaculately tailored suit and shook one loose then with old-fashioned aplomb, struck a match torn from a fancy embossed book and lit it; savoured the smoke and hissed a breath out.

"You might think I've brought you here because I'm angry, Lena, but I'm not. I'm just very disappointed."

A shuddering, heaving sob wracked the girl, her eyes screwed tight in pain. Millar reached out and tenderly touched her tear-streaked cheek.

He tore off the strip of cloth tape. It dangled from the left side of her mouth, the glue tearing a strip of skin from her lips, which bloomed fresh blood.

"Mr Mi-llar...!" Pleading. Her once pretty face, swollen, the eyes of a seasoned pugilist, lips split, one canine broken. Bloody and ugly with fear and pain.

"Shush, now, Lena. I don't expect you to say anything. The time for that will come later." Millar drew on the cigarette, tip flaring. He tapped dead ash into his palm.

"All this savagery Gary dished out is nothing to what's coming, my love. Downstairs there's a dozen coked-up horny wee bastards who are going to take turns with you. They'll not be gentle like I always insisted our friends were. No privileges of rank now, lady. There'll be no posh frocks or fancy apartment. No luxury hotel rooms and magnums of Bolly for you..." The words were spoken softly, soothing. No sharpness or edge. Almost a lullaby. Leaning forward, he put the lit cigarette to the girl's thigh.

She screamed, rocking in the chair but unable to writhe away because of the tight bindings. The screams died to whimpers and tears rolled down her cheeks.

Millar inhaled another long draw, then waved the red tip.

"That little tantrum has upset some very influential friends of mine. Generous friends. Your problem is you've gotten too big for your Jimmy Choo's."

Peeling the rest of the tape away, he gazed into her bloodshot eyes. He could still see beauty there amid the terror.

Millar exploded into motion, lashing out with a sharp

backhand that drew an intake of breath from the woman. Before she could look up, his chair scraped back and he savagely punched her in the mouth. The force knocked the chair over. Her head slammed into the floor and she mewled a high whine. He snarled over her, face contorted in rage.

"That bloody scene lost me thousands! I'm going to have you broke back in, miss. It might teach you your place again." Millar was breathing heavily, enraged.

"You're going to be shackled to that table like a piece of fucking meat and when they've all had their fill, then I'm coming back in here with a broken pool cue and…"

"And you'll what?"

Millar spun around at the unexpected sound of the voice. His senses coalescing together in a blur to take in the image.

Male. Six foot. Athletic. The fabric of the black technical sweatshirt strained across broad shoulders. Narrow waist. Hiking trousers, black again over dark boots. Military boots. High over the ankle. Leather and synthetic mesh. No noise as he stepped forward. Slight limp.

Dark eyes below a black ski mask. Sawn-off shotgun trained in both hands. Practised tactical movement.

"Who the fuck are you? Have you any idea who you're…"

"Shut it and drop the gun. I know who I'm dealing with." Voice calm, a nod towards Millar's concealed weapon.

"You think I need to pull the gun? I'm telling you once more, sunshine, you can fuck off now and you might have a chance, but in about thirty seconds this room's going to be filled with boys who'll cut you to shreds very fucking slowly.

That's after they give you a piece of what this bitch will be getting. They're not fussy, you see. I hope you like a bit of rough." Millar squared up to the stranger, chin jutted. The whining girl behind him was now silent; eyes wide at the intrusion.

Millar pointed a defiant finger.

"I'm going to give you the count of…"

BOOM.

The squeal was unnatural. It took the full second for Millar to realise it was his own. Lena's terrified screams added to the chaos as she rocked and bucked in the overturned chair.

Millar looked down at his right arm.

The close-up blast had shredded the hand to a broken twist of meat and torn the flexor and extensor muscles of the forearm to shreds; the white of shattered radius and ulna stark against the pulsing blood which was pooling on the floor at his feet at an alarming rate. Radial artery catastrophically severed by the broken bones. His useless lower arm now hanging perpendicular to its upper half. His chest peppered with dots of blood. White shirt beginning to bloom red in slow motion.

Shocked but moving from primal instinct, Millar reached for the revolver tucked into a speed holster concealed on the waistband of his trousers.

BOOM.

The room kicked out from under him. Unbearable pain as hundreds of tiny hornets shattered his kneecap and peppered through flesh to splinter the femur. The revolver skittered across the floor.

Senses dulling, Millar watched as the intruder dumped the shotgun and turned away to push two wooden wedges under the door and give them a kick for good measure. Millar recognised now the weapon was Rowdy's, the butt bloody, which meant aid may not be as forthcoming as first thought.

Groaning, he attempted to drag himself towards his own discarded gun.

A heavy boot to his shattered knee ended any ambition of retaliation in a gasp of howling agony. The figure loomed over him. Dark eyes stared into his own. Millar coughed, felt the coppery taste of blood in his mouth.

Hauled from the floor and dragged across the room, he was unceremoniously dumped on the old sofa.

"You're bleeding out. You don't have long so stop struggling."

Millar choked, blood in his mouth as he tried to raise his shattered arm and push back against the man.

"You need to focus on the next few minutes. It's over, Rab." A gloved fist twisted the fabric of his collar.

Rab Millar stared at the surreal form of his shattered limb oozing deep red blood into the filthy sofa. His lower leg twisted at an unnatural angle. A slap across the face. The man's eyes bore into him. Familiar eyes. A string of bloody drool ran onto his ruined two hundred quid shirt.

"You'll regret…"

The breath was blasted from his broken body as a flurry of heavy right-handed punches battered his solar plexus.

Gasping, Millar flopped back onto the battered sofa, the masked face close to his own.

"You thought you'd got away with it, didn't you? That the truth was buried. Well, the game's up, Rab. For all of you."

Thompson snapped off his nitrile gloves and dropped them in a bin.

"Don't be distracted by the rest of the damage. He died as a direct result of blood loss from the gunshot wounds. Frightful mess it made too. Shotgun. Close range. Severed both the radial and ulnar arteries. It nearly took off his lower leg too. You have the weapon?"

"Recovered at the scene," Macpherson confirmed.

The assistant was bagging items of clothing that had been cut off and was storing them away. Once the next of kin had been informed then the butchery could begin in earnest. Stainless steel trays would be filled with organs, and samples taken during the PM would be assessed to determine Millar's blood alcohol levels and any traces of drugs in his system, amongst other things. Not that it was likely to conclude anything different. A small silver dish lay heavy with its little load of deformed black pellets plucked from torn flesh; a gruesome caviar of bloody buckshot.

"We'll have the full report prepared and passed across to you as soon as it's complete, but that's the summation."

"Thanks."

"So, shall we call this one a happy accident?" said Macpherson. Taylor stood nearby, a frown focused on the corpse.

"I never thought I'd see the day it caught up to him."

"You know him?" Thompson's surgical gown and mask had followed the gloves into the trash. He beckoned them to follow him from the cutting room.

"Rab Millar." Taylor nodded.

The conversation was brief as they made their way to his office.

"If there was a villain of the year, then your man was a contender," said Macpherson.

"Live by the sword, die by the sword or in this case two point-blank, twelve-gauge, number five shot," Thompson philosophised, a hand holding his door for the officers to follow.

There was a whiteboard hung by the entrance. No messages, but a game of hangman underway. Little head and neck. One arm stencilled in blue erasable marker. Ten letters. _ _ _ _O, _ _O, I, _. The letters A and E already scratched out beneath the gallows.

His office was every inch the lair of the busy professional, and he gestured towards two chairs for the visitors. Clearing a rough space on his desk, he dropped his notes, fishing under a pile of loose papers for his phone and checked it for messages. A list of contact numbers and anatomy charts were pinned to the wall, and a bookcase sagged under the weight of medical manuals and periodicals. A mug declaring 'I'd find you more interesting if you were dead' sat beside a grinning skull, bookended by a photograph of a younger Thompson and an elderly woman, and framed diplomas.

"You'll have dealt with some of his handiwork in the last nine months," said Taylor.

"Is that so?"

"The Ballyskeagh drowning and the unlawful death in Brookvale."

"The one with the broken baseball bat?"

Taylor confirmed it was with a dip of her head.

"Couldn't get charges to stick. Slippery as an eel that one," said Macpherson.

"His chequered history has in very brutal fashion caught up with him then," said Thompson, as he put his phone away. "Do you think his death may connect to one of those?" The professor scribbled a ballpoint pen on the back of a legal pad, discarding it for another when it failed to write.

"I'm ruling nothing out. We know he had involvement not just in dealing, but also in the trafficking of drugs and young women which would automatically put him in the firing line of competitors and opportunists," said Taylor. "My gut also says Millar was managing affairs for Gordon Beattie during his absence."

"Gordon Beattie, the acquittal last month? The Concrete King?"

"That one. Yes."

"Slippery as an oily eel. Bought his way out of it more like," said Macpherson.

"We also suspect Robert Millar of making some of Beattie's problems disappear."

"Under the patio." The sergeant mimed a digging action.

"It's fair to say Millar had many a secret stashed away and we've just lost the chance to hear them," added Taylor.

"On the plus side though, perhaps a happy accident as Sergeant Macpherson suggests," said Thompson.

"One way of looking at it. The chief constable will want to avoid another feud flaring up over the head of it though," said Taylor. "Our superintendent is already having a coronary at the budgetary waste in failing to bring down Beattie without throwing more resources at keeping the firms apart."

"It was messy and has the hallmarks of an execution. You have a suspect coming into the main hospital for treatment?"

Taylor half nodded.

"Why look a gift horse in the mouth, eh?"

Taylor hesitated and shot a glance towards her detective sergeant.

"We'll be treating her as a witness," she said.

"I see."

"She's seven stone soaking wet and the initial assessment was she had been taped to a chair and beaten. She's in a bad way."

"Complicates things." Thompson's brows rose above a pair of half-moon glasses he had perched on his nose.

"There's every chance, any other day of the week, we would have found that wee girl spread out on some ghetto wasteland with a bag over her head and a bullet in her skull," said Macpherson.

Taylor was once again perusing the initial crime scene

photographs that had been snapped, uploaded and printed out. Studying the level of ferocity. The efficiency of it. She couldn't put her finger on what troubled her exactly.

"We're going to need a fast track on any evidence left behind on the body, please. Diane Pearson and her team will be ripping apart the club for the same." Thompson's expression was one of accedence.

"Beattie has had a few more pressing distractions, which means he might not have as much of an iron grip as he would like. This could be as simple as someone making sure any of Rab Millar's recent antics were punished or a land grab by a competitor of Beattie. We need a lead because whoever did this and whatever group they're part of, we can't have reprisals and more bodies stacking up."

"Aye, no matter how grateful we are," mumbled Macpherson.

CODE OF SILENCE is out now on Amazon Kindle and Kindle Unlimited

AUTHORS NOTE

I AM GRATEFUL now that the dark days known as the troubles are in the distant past and as a society, while not perfect, we have moved on.

My books explore these new times where the police and law enforcement face dynamic changing threats and challenges while still dealing with the shadow of the past.

I hope that my version of the city and my novels and characters can open this great place up to a new audience who will love its flawed uniqueness as much as I do.

Belfast and Northern Ireland as a whole has so much to offer and when we come together to showcase our diversity, shared love of friendship, family and strangers for a small speck of green in a very big world we shine very brightly indeed.

I hope during these difficult times those who can visit will, and when the world gets back to normal, global pandemics return to their place in dystopian fiction novels and travel restrictions are lifted, many more international travellers can experience the world renowned craic and hospitality of this

once troubled but always welcoming island we here know
as :

       'The Land of the Giants.'

Get Exclusive Material

GET EXCLUSIVE NEWS AND UPDATES FROM THE AUTHOR

Building a relationship with my readers is *the* best thing about writing.

Visit and join up for information on new books and deals and to find out more about my life growing up on the same streets that Detective Inspector Taylor treads, you will receive the exclusive e-book 'IN/FAMOUS' containing an in-depth interview and a selection of True Crime stories about the flawed but fabulous city that inspired me to write.

You can get this **for free,** by signing up at my website.

Visit at www.pwjordanauthor.com

About Phillip Jordan

ABOUT PHILLIP JORDAN

Phillip Jordan was born in Belfast, Northern Ireland and grew up in the city that holds the dubious double honour of being home to Europe's Most Bombed Hotel and scene of its largest ever bank robbery.

He had a successful career in the Security Industry for twenty years before transitioning into the Telecommunications Sector.

Aside from writing Phillip has competed in Olympic and Ironman Distance Triathlon events both Nationally and Internationally including a European Age-Group Championship and the World Police and Fire Games.

Taking the opportunity afforded by recent world events to write full-time Phillip wrote his Debut Crime Thriller, CODE OF SILENCE, finding inspiration in the dark and tragic history of Northern Ireland but also in the black humour, relentless tenacity and Craic of the people who call the fabulous but flawed City of his birth home.

* * *

Phillip now lives on the County Down coast and is currently
writing two novel series.
For more information:
www.pwjordanauthor.com
www.facebook.com/phillipjordanauthor/

Copyright

Cover Image- Shutterstock

FIVE FOUR PUBLISHING

Printed in Great Britain
by Amazon